KAY THOMPSON'S

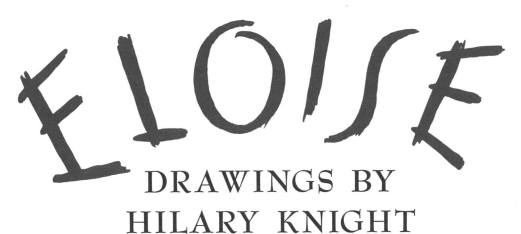

ELOISE

DRAWINGS BY
HILARY KNIGHT

A BOOK FOR PRECOCIOUS GROWN UPS

Simon & Schuster Books for Young Readers

SIMON & SCHUSTER BOOKS FOR YOUNG READERS
AN IMPRINT OF SIMON & SCHUSTER CHILDREN'S
PUBLISHING DIVISION
1230 AVENUE OF THE AMERICAS
NEW YORK, NEW YORK 10020
COPYRIGHT © 1955 BY KAY THOMPSON
COPYRIGHT RENEWED 1983 BY KAY THOMPSON
ALL RIGHTS RESERVED INCLUDING THE RIGHT OF
REPRODUCTION IN WHOLE OR IN PART IN ANY FORM.
SIMON & SCHUSTER BOOKS FOR YOUNG READERS IS A
TRADEMARK OF SIMON & SCHUSTER
0615 LAK
ISBN 978-0-671-22350-2
LIBRARY OF CONGRESS CATALOG CARD NUMBER 55-11039
MANUFACTURED IN THE UNITED STATES OF AMERICA

70 69 68 67 66 65 64 63

I am Eloise

I am six

I am a city child
I live at The Plaza

There is a lobby which is enormously large
with marble pillars and ladies in it and a revolving
door with 𝖕𝖕 on it

I spend an awful lot of time in the lobby
For instance every day I have to go to the
Desk Clerk and see what's happening there

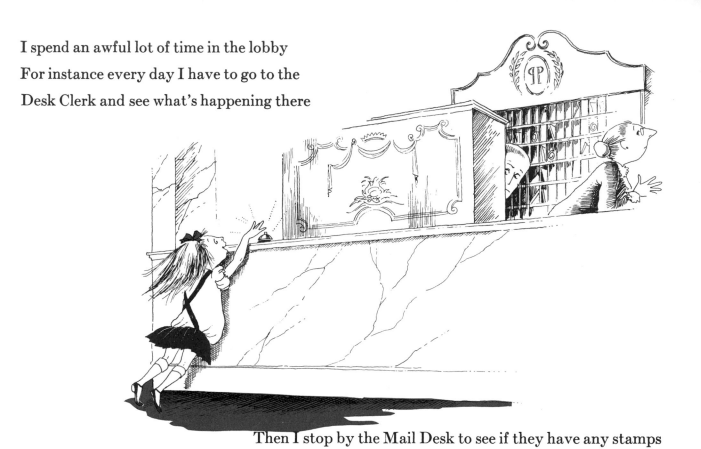

Then I stop by the Mail Desk to see if they have any stamps

Then I go to the House Phones
and make several calls to see
if anybody's in

The Bell Captain knows who I am

If there is a lot of luggage trying to get in the elevator
and these people are all in a crowd and smoking and from
out of town or something, I edge into the middle of it and
lose my skate key

I am a nuisance in the lobby
Mr. Salomone said so
He is the Manager
I always say "Good morning, Mr. Salomone"
and he always says "Good morning, Eloise"

My mother knows The Owner

I live on the top floor

Of course I am apt to be on any floor at any time

And if I want to go anywhere I simply take the elevator

For instance if I happen to be on the second floor I just

press that button until it comes up and as soon as that

door is open I get in and say *"5th floor* please" and

when those doors clank shut we ride up and I get out on

the *5th floor* and as soon as that elevator is out of

sight I skibble up those stairs to the *8th floor* and then

I press that button and when that same elevator comes up and

as soon as that door is open I get in and say *"15th floor*

please" and then when those doors clank shut we ride up

and I get out on the *15th floor* and as soon as that elevator

is out of sight I skibble down to the *12th floor* and press

that button and when that same elevator comes up and those

doors open I say *"The Lobby* please" and then those doors

clank shut and we ride down without saying absolutely one word

and then I get into the next elevator and go all the way up.

Then I get off at the top floor

And look in the mirror at me

ELOISE

END
HERE

UP

BEGIN
HERE

I live down at the end of the hall

Sometimes I take two sticks and skidder them along the walls

And when I run down the hall I slomp my feet against the woodwork which is very good for scuffing and noise

Sometimes I slomp my skates if I want to make a really loud and terrible racket

17

We have a buzzer on our front door

I always lean on it

That's how Nanny knows it's me

ELOISE

Nanny is my nurse

She wears tissue paper in her dress

and you can hear it

She is English and has 8 hairpins

made out of bones

She says that's all she needs in

this life for Lord's sake

Nanny says she would rawther I didn't

talk talk talk all the time

She always says everything 3 times

like Eloise you cawn't cawn't cawn't

Sometimes I hit her on the ankle with a tassel

She is my mostly companion

I have my own room

It has a coat rack which is as large as me

21

I have a dog that looks like a cat

His name is Weenie

Sometimes I put sunglasses on him

22   Then I have to scratch his back with a wire hanger

I have a turtle

His name is Skipperdee

He eats raisins and wears sneakers

The Plaza is the only hotel in New York

that will allow you to have a turtle

Skipperdee and me we always know its morning

because Weenie breathes in our face and kisses us

The absolutely first thing I have to do

is braid Skipperdee's ears

Otherwise he gets cross and develops a rash

Nanny gets up feeling tired tired tired

and puts on her kimono

and skibbles over to slam those windows

down shut so that we don't

freeze freeze freeze

Then she stretches her muscles

and feels fresh fresh fresh

Nanny yawns out loud

Then I pick up the telephone

and call Room Service

Ooooooooo I absolutely love Room Service

They always know its me

and they say "Yes, Eloise?"

And I always say "Hello, this is me ELOISE and would you

kindly send one roast-beef bone, one raisin and seven spoons

to the top floor and charge it please

Thank you very much"

Then I hang up and look at the ceiling

for a while and think of a

way to get a present

I usually yawn out loud several times

Then Nanny gives the signal and Weenie and Skipperdee and me

we skibble out of bed as fast as everly we can and Nanny wraps

us in our robe and holds us tight

And I pat her on her botto

which is large

Then we have to do our morning duties and laugh and sing

London from bottom to top is zup

The keeper in the shop is zup

And even Mrs. Mop is zup

Oh what a love-a-ly mawning

In Trafalgar Square the Bobby's zup

In Piccadilly the Nippy's zup

In Covent Garden the Clippy's zup

Oh what a love-a-ly mawning

We're zup and we've got to be jolly clean

From head to toe and in between

Zup good morning and how've ya been

Oh what a love-a-ly mawning

The Royal Navy is up-is-zup

Buckingham Palace is up-is-zup

And even the BBC is-zup

Oh what a love-a-ly

Oh what a love-a-ly

Oh what a love-a-ly mawning

The Roy-al Na-vy is up-is-zup Buck-ing-ham Pal-ace is

up-is-zup And e-ven the B B C is-zup Oh what a love-a-ly

Oh what a love-a-ly Oh what a love-a-ly maw — ning

Ooooooooo I just love Nanny I absolutely do

While I'm brushing my teeth there is this pigeon who is always
hanging around our bathroom window and he does absolutely nothing
but coo
He is fat and grisly and I holler at him and he
flies over to the Sherry-Netherland for a while to see what they're
up to

Weenie and me weigh 36
Nanny weighs 18 stones

Skipperdee weighs absolutely nothing at all
unless he has his sneakers on
Then of course he weighs ½

Then Nanny puts on her corset which is

enormously large but which is very good for her back

Kleenex makes a very good hat

When we are clean we skibble in our scuffs to the kitchen

and there is René with Room Service

René always says "Bonjour, Eloise, voici votre petit déjeuner"

Nanny always says "My my my doesn't that look good!"

And I always say "Bonjour, René, merci and charge it please

Nanny has Irish bacon
which reminds her of her brother

You have to eat oatmeal or you'll dry up
Anybody knows that

Nanny likes her coffee hot hot hot
An egg cup makes a very good hat

31

I have two dolls which is enough

Their names are Sabine and Saylor

Sabine is a rag doll and she has absolutely no face at all

partially because she came from Jamaica by Air Express

Otherwise she has shoe-button eyes and two right legs

She is *rawther* unusual

Saylor is a very large doll and has a hard head and no arms

She was in the most terriblest accident and she bleeded so hard

she almost choked in the night and this ambulance came and took

her to this hospital and it was an emergency and they had to give

her all this terribly dark medicine and a lot of Band-aids and when

she came back home she was weak weak weak and had to take cod-liver

oil

I gave her a strawberry leaf from under my grapefruit for not

whimpering and Weenie licked her face

They have to have a teaspoon of water every hour or so, so you can

see they are an extremely lot of extra work

Here's what I like to do

Make things up

Here's what I can do

Chew gum

Write

Spell

Stand on my head for the longest amount of time

34

Stand on my toes

Get dizzy and fall down

Make a terrible face

And here's the thing of it

Most of the time I'm on the telephone

My day is rawther full

I have to call the Valet and tell him

to get up here and pick up

my sneakers to be cleaned and pressed

and have them back for

sure without fail

Then I have to play the piano

and look in the mirror for a while

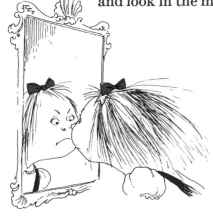

Then I have to open and close the door for a while and as

soon as I hear talking and laughing I skidder out and run down

the hall

and if there is an open door I have

to walk in and pretend I am an orphan

and sometimes I limp and sort of bend

to the side and look sort of

sad in between the arms

and they give me a piece of melon or something

Then I roam around the halls

Then I have to scurry down to
the 10th floor to adjust those
thermostats in case anyone needs it

If there's a fire on the 6th floor

I know how to fix it

Then I have to hide and see what those Hotel Officers are up to

All they do is walk and talk

I have never been arrested

Then I have to hurry back to the top floor

Our day maid's name is Johanna

She has earrings with garnets

and is going to take her Social Security

to Bavaria on her birthday

One time she saw this man in this hair net

and he bawled her out for taking his razor blades

I have to help her put on those

pillowcases or she'll never be through

by 4 for Lord's sake

She has to be through by 4

Then I have to go around to that Service Elevator on the 6th floor
and see what everybody's thrown away and if I want it or not, like
ribbon or something like that

Then I have to go down to help the Switchboard Operators
in case there are any D As and there has to be
some sort of message taken or something like that

If there is an Exit sign I always have to go into it because there might be a mattress in there and I can lie down on it and get some rest so I can carry on for Lord's sake

Oh my Lord I am absolutely so busy I don't know how I can possibly get everything done

Then I have to hop around for a while

I have lunch at the Palm Court if it is too rainy

and see Thomas

We are both rawther fond of talking and he gives

me Gugelhopfen

Thomas has a son in the Marines who got married

on a shoestring

Thomas has a Corvette

I always go in the Persian Room after 4 to see my friend Bill

He is a busboy in the night and goes to school in the day and

his eyes water

Here's where he's been

Madrid

Here's where I've been

Boiler Room

Then I scamper to the Terrace Room

where those debutantes are prancing around

Then I have to skibble into the Baroque Room because sometimes there is this chalk and there is this pitcher with ice water in it and you should see the cigar smoke left over from a General Motors meeting Oh my Lord

Then I have to help the busboys and waiters get set up in the
Crystal Room
They always wait until the last second for Lord's sake and then
we have to rush our feet off

I go to all the weddings in the White and Gold Room

and I usually stay for the reception

There are absolutely nothing but rooms in The Plaza

Ooooooooooooooooooo I absolutely love The Plaza

Sometimes if they are having this enormous affair

in the Grand Ballroom I get there early to help Joe

set up the lights in the ceiling and before anybody gets

there we just scamper up this ladder and hide up there

in those holes

Oh my Lord is it ever swelteringly hot up there

I always wear my sun visor

I am all over the hotel

Half the time I am lost

But mostly I am on the first floor because

that's where Catering is

So I have to go down there every day for at least

three hours and sometimes I have to go at night

Oh my Lord do they ever have a lot of things going on

down there

Altogether I have been to 56 affairs including Halloween

There is this Oak Room which is to the right if you want to have
a broken mint or something like that

And you have to go downstairs
to the Rendezvous Room which is
very good for hiding over a long
period of time and for doing
a tour jeté or so

The Package Room has all these packages in it and sometimes
I have to help them lift those heavy boxes and look for small
packages that might be for me ELOISE

Sometimes I go into the Men's Room which is very good for playing

Railroad Station or something like that

Every Wednesday I have to go to the Barber Shop
and have Vincent shape my hair
He does absolutely nothing but talk and swiggles
me around in that chair and hurts my neck with
that whiskbroom

Sometimes I sklonk him in the kneecap

Vincent says that if I am not careful I am not going

to have a hair on my head by the time I'm 7 for Lord's sake

Getting bored is not allowed

Sometimes I comb my hair with a fork

Sometimes I wear my arm in a sling

Sometimes I put a rubber band

on the end of my nose

Toe shoes make very good ears

Sometimes I wear them to lunch

Here's what I like to do

Pretend

Sometimes I am a mother with 40 children

Sometimes I am a giant with fire coming out of my hair

Sometimes I get terribly sick and have to be waited on

Sometimes I get so sick my head falls over and is wobbling until

it is loose

Then we have to call my mother long distance and charge it

My mother is 30 and has a charge account at Bergdorf's

She wears a 3½ shoe

I put a large cabbage leaf on my head

when I have a headache

It makes a very good hat

My mother knows Coco Chanel

50

She goes to Europe and to Paris

and sends for me if there's some sun

I am always packed in case I have to leave on TWA

at a moment's notice or something like that

My mother has A T & T stock and she knows an ad man

whatever that is

Sometimes my mother goes to Virginia

with her lawyer

He has an office on Madison Avenue

He has already had the whooping

cough and the measles

Sometimes I give him rubber candy

He is absolutely so dumb he eats it

Sometimes he brings me a present

whether I deserve it or not

I usually do

Here's what he likes

Martinis

Here's what I like

Dandelions

But not very often

I absolutely dislike school

so Philip is my tutor

He goes to Andover

My mother knows the Dean

He wears red garters and is boring boring boring

When we have our French lesson he reads in French about la petite cousine de Marie and her jardin and sometimes I listen to him but not very often

Here's what makes Philip angry

He says "Alors! nous commençerons" and I say "Alors! nous commencerons"

And he says "Shall we settle down Eloise? And I say "Shall we settle down Eloise?"

And he says "That's quite enough Eloise"

And I say "That's quite enough Eloise"

And he says "I mean it Eloise"

And I say "I mean it Eloise" right back at him

And he looks at me with fiercely eyes

And I look right back at him with fiercely eyes

And then he says "That will do Eloise"

And then I say "That will do Eloise"

And then he shouts "Eloise I mean it"

And then I shout "Eloise I mean it" right after him

And then he gets madder and says "Stop it at once Eloise"

And then I say "Stop it at once Eloise"

And then he stands up and says "Very well Eloise"

And then I stand up and say "Very well Eloise"

And then he walks around the room

And then I walk around the room

And then he screams "Nanny"

Then I scream "Nanny"

And Nanny comes in yelling "Non non non Eloise" and she claps her hands and Skipperdee and me we skibble over and hide behind the television or fall dead behind a hidden door

And then Nanny puts her arm around Philip and calls Room Service and says "Send three of everything please"

And when the waiter brings the check Nanny signs my mother's name

And I simply tell him to "charge it please and thank you very much"

Then I do a cartwheel

Philip is always glad to go home

Every night I have to call Room Service to send up that menu

so we can order our dinner for Lord's sake

I always have to read it for a few seconds or so

Then I just say "I'll have the Planked Medallion of Beef Tenderloin

with Fresh Vegetables Maison please and two raisins, one strawberry

leaf and one clams in season s'il vous plaît and charge it please

Thank you very much"

Ooooooooooooooooo I absolutely love Room Service

The night maid's name is Lily

She married the engineer of the subway and cut her hair

but I think she's sorry

She gives us extra pillowcases and soap

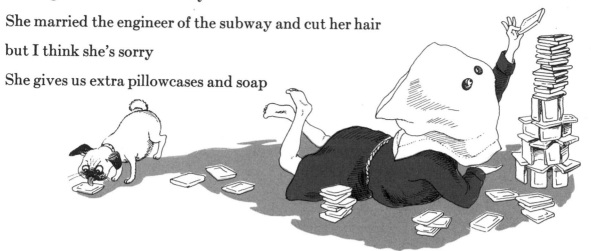

Once there was this most terriblest storm that came up and

it rained and all this thunder was clomping itself into

this water and all these people were drowning without air

Absolutely no one was saved

Paper cups are very good for talking to Mars

TV is in the Drawing Room

I always watch it with my parasol in case there's some sort of glare

And oh my Lord when it's fight night Nanny is absolutely wild and we

have to scamper into our places and get ready and Nanny has to find

her Players and I have to get my binoculars and call Room Service

and order three Pilsener Beers for Nanny and one meringue glacée

for me ELOISE and charge it please

Thank you very much

Here's what I hate

Howdy Doody

Ooooooooooooooooooo I absolutely love TV

Every night when it's time to go to bed Nanny yawns out loud

and says she is tired tired tired

I make as much noise as I possibly can like turning on the phonograph

real loud and hollering a lot

Then I have to brush Nanny's hair
for her
And then we both yawn out loud and
get into our pajamas

Then I have to put on my Don't Disturb sign and get Skipperdee and

Weenie and me all tucked in and then Nanny opens the windows

enormously wide so we can have air air air

Then she turns out the light

Nanny has a mole   61

Sometimes we go to sleep right away

But not very often

Sometimes Weenie and Skipperdee and me we get out of bed and go
into that closet and look around for a while and when we get in there
there is this cave and it is so dark in there that it's absolutely black
and there is this big bug in there that has those enormously large
feathers and he picks us up by our necks and sklanks us around in his
paws and carries us down into this deep well that is all filled with
tigers and lions and birds of prey and they eat us up raw and step
on us and stamp their feet on us and absolutely rank us

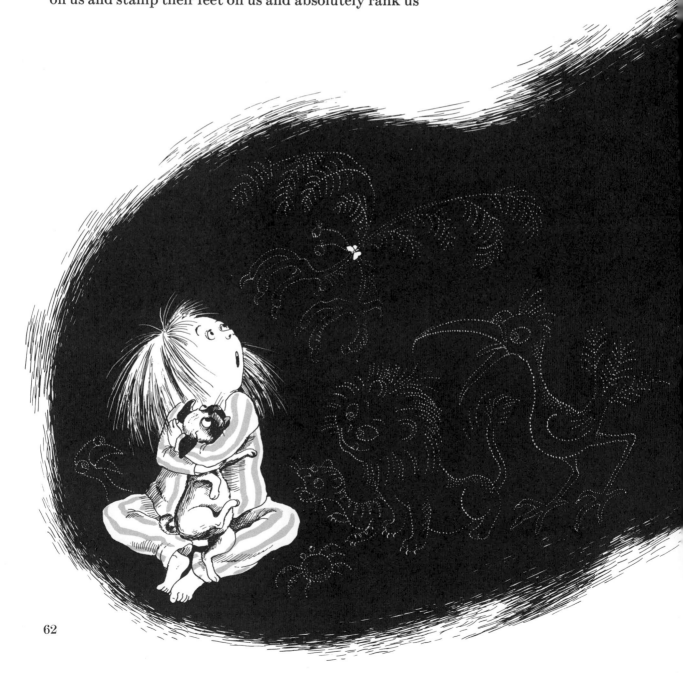

and we have to run for our lives and drag each other on our stomach
and scrape our face along the side until we are absolutely breathing
and stretching our arms to reach that closet door barely in time
and our heart is beating and we have to wake Nanny with a flashlight
in her face to save us and put witch hazel and cotton on all of our
toenails

And Nanny has to get up and pamper me and spoil me for a while

while I am out of my head with fever and pain

After all I am only 6

There's so much to do

Tomorrow I think I'll pour a pitcher of water down the mail chute

Ooooooooooooooooooooo I absolutely love The Plaza